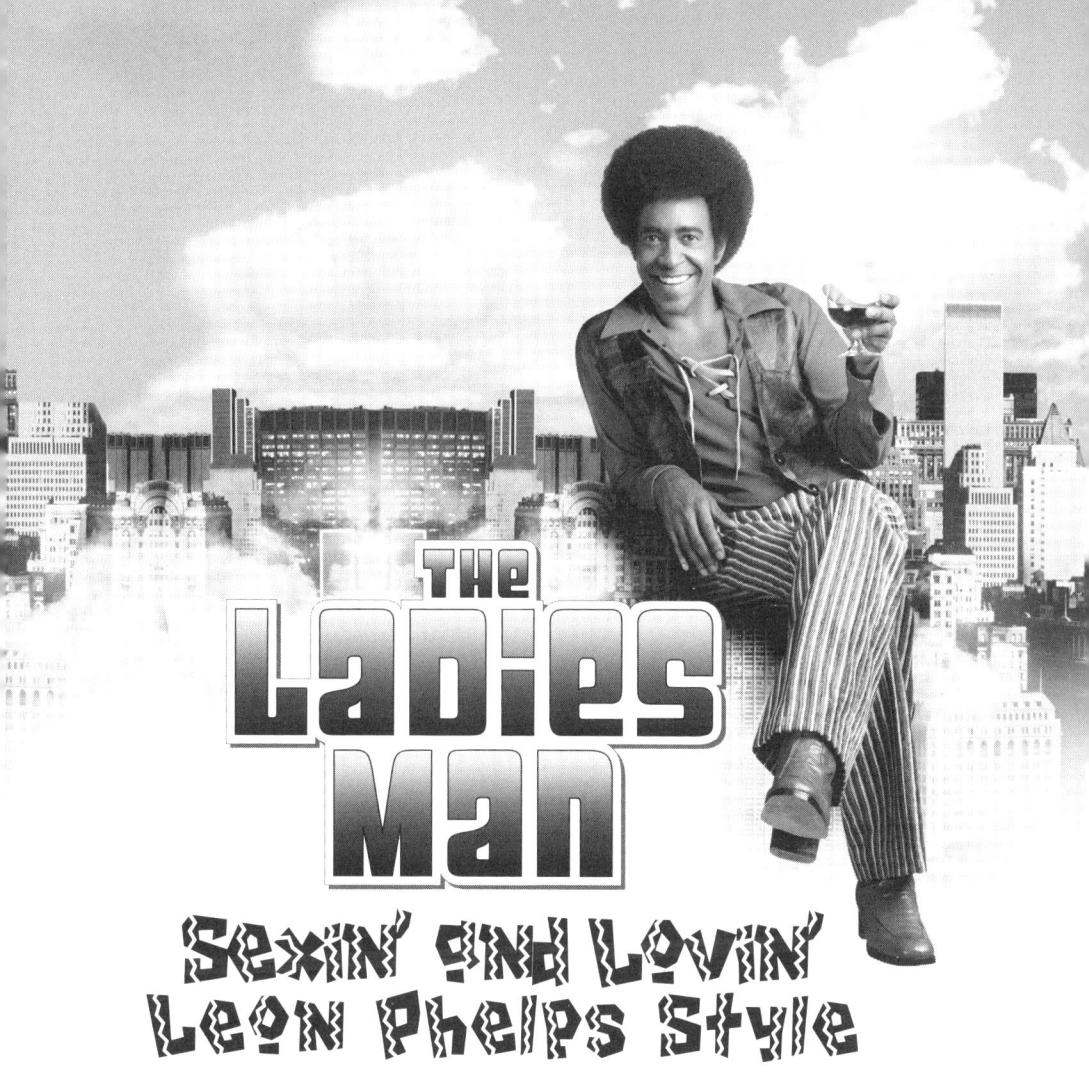

THE LADIES MAN

Sexin' and Lovin' Leon Phelps Style

Andrew Steele & Dennis McNicholas
with Tim Meadows

TV Books
NEW YORK

TM & COPYRIGHT © 2000 BY PARAMOUNT PICTURES
TM & COPYRIGHT © 2000 BY NBC ENTERPRISES, INC.
ALL RIGHTS RESERVED.

All rights reserved. No part of this book may be reproduced in any form or by any means without permission in writing from the publishers, except by a reviewer who may quote brief passages in a review.

TV Books, L.L.C.
1619 Broadway, Ninth Floor
New York, NY 10019
www.tvbooks.com

Interior and cover design by Daly Design.

Illustrations by Corky McCoy. McCoy has been an art director/illustrator for thirty years. He was art director for Miles Davis from 1975 through 1988, creating many of Mr. Davis's album covers and other original art. He is currently working on a book titled **A View of Miles**.

Manufactured in the United States of America.

Contents

Introduction:
Do You Have What It Takes to Be a Ladies Man?   9

Sweet Talkin
How to Talk Like the Ladies Man, Leon Phelps   16

Leon's Advisor   19

How to Dress Like the Ladies Man   27

Cocktail Recipes   33

Love Makin'
She Will, If   38

She Won't, If   39

Leon's Medical History   40

Leon's Night on the Town for Just $3.98   46

Forms of Contraception   54

Selected Excerpts from Leon's Little Black Book   59

Killin' Time
Leon's Berlitz Guide to Worldwide Conquest   66

Leon's Five Sexiest Novels   68

Introduction

DO YOU HAVE WHAT IT TAKES TO BE A LADIES MAN?

his here simple quiz is designed to help you, the reader, determine if you have the wangular mettle—that's scientifically speakin'—to be a ladies man such as one not dissimilar from yours truly, Leon Phelps, the Ladies Man. Obviously, this test is for men, but if you are a lady (a lady!), I encourage you to take it as well because I find that very sexy and dirty in a stimulating way.

1. YOU TYPICALLY MAKE LOVE FOR . . .
    a) 7 hours
    b) 9 hours
    c) 12 hours
    d) 14 hours

2. YOUR FAVORITE PLACE TO MEET WOMEN IS . . .
   a) a bar
   b) the bus station
   c) a convenience store, in the back by the Funyuns® rack
   d) in your bed, after making love to them

3. YOUR BEST PICK-UP LINE IS . . .
   a) "My name is Leon Phelps."
   b) "Hey, baby, do you believe in love at first sight, or should I put it back in my pants?"
   c) "I'm real sorry about givin' you VD that time. Let me make it up to you, baby."
   d) "Hey, baby, why don't you lose the zero and let me do it in the butt?"

4. YOUR FAVORITE PART OF MAKING LOVE IS . . .
 a) snuggling
 b) doing it
 c) the butt
 d) the ass

5. YOU KNOW THAT IT'S TIME TO END A RELATIONSHIP WHEN . . .
 a) the love makin' has come to an end
 b) you've reached the point in the relationship where familiarity gives way to routine
 c) the bus station is closing
 d) Yeah, "relationship." Now what is that?

6. YOU'RE FAVORITE PET NAME FOR A LADY IS . . .
 a) Skank
 b) Ho
 c) Skank-Ho
 d) Typically, "names" don't play a large part in what we doin'.

7. SHE WANTS YOU TO HAVE DINNER WITH HER PARENTS, SO YOU . . .
 a) smile and agree with everything her father says
 b) suggest that maybe her parents would like to see how talented and flexible their daughter is
 c) don't let her father see your hand on her mother's fine and shapely butt
 d) tell her mother that she's gotta quiet down—there are people in the stall next door

8. YOUR FAVORITE SEXUAL POSITION IS . . .
   a) the missionary position
   b) in the bus station
   c) behind the Waffle House
   d) "The Alabama Crab Dangle"

9. YOUR FAVORITE PART OF A WOMAN'S BODY IS . . .
   a) the butt
   b) the booty
   c) the ass
   d) her self-esteem

10. WHEN YOU ARE MAKIN' LOVE, YOU ARE THINKING ABOUT . . .
    a) how you will escape when her trucker husband comes home
    b) Delta Burke
    c) how the Microsoft anti-trust trial is going to affect the state of free trade in our post-NAFTA economy
    d) the butt

11. YOU CONSIDER YOUR BEST PERSONALITY TRAIT TO BE YOUR . . .
    a) sense of humor
    b) excellent taste in fine, French sippin' cognacs (I think you know what I mean)
    c) Afrosheen
    d) superior wang

12. You feel naked without your . . .
    a) Cool Water cologne
    b) zodiac sign medallion
    c) Black Power Fist Afro pick
    d) I am naked right now.

13. No lovemakin' session is complete without . . .
    a) a bottle of Courvoisier
    b) High Karate-scented love candles
    c) A heavy-duty, all-weather edition of the "Kama Sutra"
    d) payin' the bill

14. YOUR FAVORITE "MARITAL AID" IS . . .
   a) ginseng
   b) Ben-Wa balls
   c) a superior wang
   d) "Designing Women" reruns

15. YOU ARE ABOUT TO MAKE LOVE AND FIND YOURSELF UNABLE TO PERFORM SO YOU . . .
   a) politely apologize
   b) wake up screaming
   c) get right with the Lord because the Apocalypse is upon us
   d) Unable to perform?! Yeah. Now what is that?

SCORING

In the time that it has taken you to complete this test, I have already romanced nearly seven very skanky young ladies, proving that the winner of this test is none other than yours truly, Leon Phelps, the Ladies Man.

Caller #1: Yes, uh, Ladies Man. I...I have a problem. I'm having a hard time finding the right lady. I've dated a few, but none of them are hot enough. I've got to have a hot lady.

Leon: [laughing] Yeah, I know what you mean, yeah! Uh, might I suggest that you try lowering your standards, you know? Because, really, we all would like to date a supermodel, or a fine lady, like, uh, Delta Burke. You know? But, uh, that may not always be possible, and that is why God invented the skank.

You say:	The Ladies Man says:
PENIS	WANG
SEXUAL INTERCOURSE	WANG TIME
FEMALE GENITALIA	WANG CENTER
BREASTS	FUN BAGS
BUTT	YEAH, I LIKE THAT.
BEDROOM	HUMPATORIUM
EJACULATE	WANG
RESTAURANT	HUMPATORIUM
DELTA BURKE	RAISON D'ETRE
GREAT	HORNY
SEXUAL INTERCOURSE	DANCIN' THE WANGO
1978 GMC EL CAMINO	MOBILE HUMPATORIUM
IMPOTENCE	?????
ERECTION	GETTIN' WANGRY
FANTASTIC	HORNY
A DUMPSTER	HUMPATORIUM
BETTER THAN AVERAGE	HORNY
WOMAN	LADY
LADY	SKANK
SKANK	SKANK
BUS STATION SKANK	BUS STATION SKANK
GAS STATION SKANK	GAS STATION SKANK
SEXUAL INTERCOURSE	MISTRESS OF MY PASSIONS
MAN	WALKIN' THE WANG PLANK
THE PENTAGON	WANGLO-AMERICAN
AMAZING	HUMPATORIUM
HORNY	HORNY
LUBRICANT	CONSCIOUS
PENIS	WANG GLIDER
	MR. BOWANGLES

LEON'S ADVISOR

Cars

The converted van is truly the Cadillac of automobiles. Complete with shag carpeting, black lights, day-glo paint, mirrors, a disco ball, a four-speaker sound system, eight-track tape deck, and fine Corinthian vinyl interior, this hump truck is the envy of weekend Wanglists everywhere. Let me say personally that when my friend Martell lets me borrow his Mobile Ass-ault Unit it becomes a veritable Venus Lady Trap or, at the very least, a Lady Pitcher Plant.

Stereos

Like a tender lover whispering sweet nothings through the darkness, this compact system will give you endless aural pleasure as you let the AM band provide the private soundtrack to your very own "Quiet Storm." Hands down, the most seductive feature of this high and tight little beauty is its multi-tasking ability—not only can you woo your sweet lady, but if programmed properly this device can also serve as a clock and an alarm. Sometimes there's nothing sexier than utility.

Liquors

ourvoisier. Would you expect anything less?

Cologne

igh Karate. One whiff of this most erotic of stenches is enough to drive most ladies to the brink of crotchular meltdown. If by some unfortunate chance you cannot procure this semi-mythical love elixir, I invite you to dip a wet nap in some Hawaiian Punch and rub it liberally about your neck and torso. I guarantee that your lady will be none the wiser.

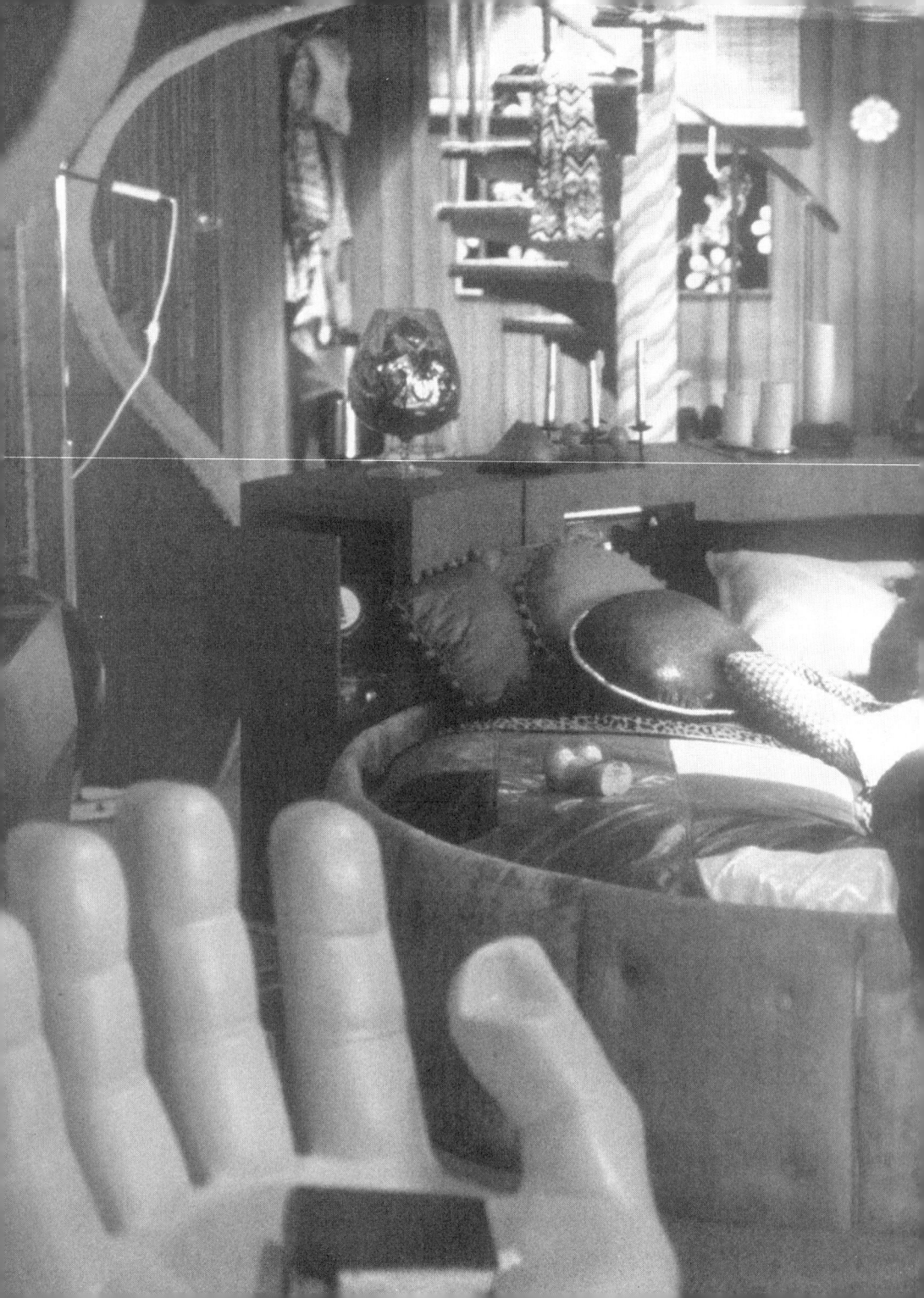

Art

The "Kama Sutra." Aesthetically pleasing and thoroughly informative, this objet d'art is a must for any salon d'hump. The addition of a black light not only unlocks the erotic mysteries of the Orient but also your lover's thighs.

Martell: So, whatchoo gonna be doing then, bro?

Leon Phelps: Well, um, I don't want to get into the particulars, um... but I know that a bottle of Courvoisier and a lady will definitely be involved. You know what I mean?

HOW TO DRESS LIKE THE LADIES MAN

Hair

The first thing that a woman notices about a man after the protuberance in his groinological vicinity is, undoubtedly, his silky, highly strokable coiffure. For maximum luster and body, the Ladies Man recommends high-end products such as Afrosheen. Failing that, the liberal application of any lard-based product will suffice.

Vest

Some may find it gauche to wear a synthetic leather vest like the one I am currently and perennially sporting. Find it gauche, that is, until they discover that it is but one of three pieces of an entire synthetic leather suit for which the Ladies Man paid over $48.

Shirt

The Ladies Man has found that the most important quality in fine garments is, of course, luminescence. Not only will the shiny nature of your shirt indicate the presence of a man of rare taste and sophistication, but also the generated glare can momentarily stun your average skank long enough for you to commence the sexin'. Please be advised: This type of garment is extremely flammable and the Ladies Man has the third-degree burns on his torso and upper body to prove it.

Pants

Pants are a crucial part of any ensemble as they house that most precious of cargoes, the wang. Remember that, in selecting your pants, tightness is a priority, as you do want to advertise the specific dimensions of your proverbial "man goods." However, the Ladies Man has on more than one occasion erred on the side of complete and total circulatory failure in his lower extremities. Not that

this was a bad thing, mind you, as the Ladies Man was able to parlay his potentially life-threatening wangocentric asphyxiation into an additional four hours of tender humping.

Underwear

On the highway of lovemaking, underwear is, simply put, a highly unnecessary speed bump.

Shoes

While most people select their footwear using purely stylistic criteria, the Ladies Man recommends a shoe with sufficient tread and arch support, as 80 to 90 percent of his amorous rendezvous necessitate a hasty escape via a window or fire escape from one or more pursuers who may or may not be armed.

Fragrances

Medical science has proven that certain doses of pheromones can have an aphrodisiacal effect on the ladies in close quarters. To this end, the Ladies Man has been supplementing his tried-and-true High Karate cologne with various animal extracts. While this practice has yet to pay humpatory dividends, the Ladies Man has been awoken on several occasions by different neighborhood dogs attempting maneuvers that would make even the most seasoned of bus station skanks blush.

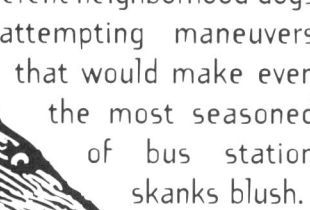

COCKTAIL RECIPES

Now, any aspiring Ladies Man should of course have several fine, high-quality cocktails in his repertoire of booty-plying tactics. While the Ladies Man is a well-known aficionado of a certain fine French sippin' cognac commonly known as Courvoisier, there are as many different cocktails as there are skanks in the world. That is to say, roughly 250. Here are five classics that are guaranteed to send your lady wangward in no time.

Martini

1 Bottle Courvoisier

2 Fancy Glasses (Optional)

Pour Courvoisier into glasses, wait for the cops to leave the bus station. Enjoy.

Gin and Tonic

1 Bottle Courvoisier

Simple and elegant, the way a true gentlemen gets his skanks drunk enough to hump.

Whiskey Sour

2 Bottles Courvoisier

This particular recipe is remarkably similar to the gin and tonic with the exception that it is slightly more potent. Before you consume this cocktail, I recommend that you hide all vacuum cleaners, jars of mayonnaise, and anything else that starts to look really attractive after seventeen or eighteen highballs.

Manhattan

1 Bottle Courvoisier

This particular beverage is best enjoyed with someone you love on a moonlit night, holding each other in a tender embrace. And then you put it in the butt.

Screwdriver

1 Bottle Courvoisier

4 Square Feet Cheesecloth

1 Garden Hose

3 Jello Molds

2 Pair Inflatable Water Wings

I think you know where I'm going with this one.

If these don't work, here are a few more that you might like to try, or, at the very least, slip to your girlfriend when she's not looking.

Between the Sheets	Sex Crime Toddy
Sex on the Beach	The Woo Woo
Screaming Orgasm	Vulva Punch
Foxy Lady	Lady of Ill Repute Cooler
Fuzzy Navel	Whore Juice
Gorilla Milk	Anal Intercourse Fizz
Monkey Gland	Manhattan Stump-Puller
Bush Ranger	Penis Whiskey
Ordinary Seaman	The Snizz
The Boob Toucher	Taint Painter
Brandy Ass Lick	Beer
Mississippi Mouth Hump	Masturbation Drink

Caller #2: Hi, Ladies Man? I'm having trouble being confident with women because I think I might be a little physically, you know, inadequate.

Leon: Inadequate, yeah. . . . Now, what is that?

Caller #2: Inferior. You know. I'm concerned about the size of my penis.

Leon: Oh-h-h, okay, yeah, now that's all right. Don't worry. The Ladies Man is here to help you. Now, um, medically speaking, just how dinky is your wang?

Caller #2: That's not very medical. Uh, two-and-a-half to three inches.

Leon: Oh, yeah, that is small. Yeah, uh, you know, I was not expecting you to say anything under ten or eleven inches. Well, I guess I was wrong, so I guess you can never really ever pleasure a woman, caller. And I'm sorry for that, but, uh, here's to you and your dinky wang, dinky wang man!

LOVE MAKIN'

She Will, If...

- She is at the bus station at 4 a.m. and does not have a ticket.
- She is drunk on beverages that are not marketed as alcohol.
- She describes one of her greatest qualities as her small teeth.
- She has the same name as a type of alcohol.
- She is trying to use food stamps to buy cigarettes.
- She has paid several thousand dollars to have her gag reflex surgically removed.
- When shown a pair of women's underwear, she points to the crotch and asks, "Why's that there?"
- She claims the smell of gasoline makes her horny.
- She has long since forgotten that whipped cream is also a dessert topping.

She Won't, If...

- At some point in the conversation, she mentions her time at college.
- Her job has little or nothing to do with carrying large numbers of dollar bills in her underwear.
- She reveals herself to be a member of law enforcement.
- She is a man.
- None of her clothes are made of fishnet.
- Her kind of dancing doesn't involve poles or songs by Van Halen.
- She does not believe that your Betamax video recorder has a direct satellite link to big Hollywood producers.
- She uses mouthwash strictly for dental hygiene.
- When she uses the name "Daddy," she is referring specifically to her father.

LEON'S MEDICAL HISTORY

he Ladies Man is proud to admit that I have contracted enough afflictions of the wang to be the subject of over twelve award-winning studies for the "New England Journal of Medicine." Some of these maladies include: genital herpes, genital herpes (simplex), chlamydia, gonorrhea, the clap, crabs, yeast infection, toxic shock syndrome, mononucleosis, hepatitis A, hepatitis B, hepatitis C, hepatitis R, drippity wang, yellow fever, consumption, scoliosis of the wang, lockjaw, gangrenous wang, botulism, bumpity wang, Japanese beetles, planter's warts, priapism, Hanta virus, elephantiasis, albinism, anthrax, dysentery, wangal distension, wang burn, tennis wang, ingrown wang, receding wangline, bipolar wang, cauliflower wang, swimmer's wang, carpal wang syndrome, water on the wang, wang shingles, wang whooping cough, phantom wang, wang tonsilitis, wang bronchitis, dutch elm wang, trick wang, trench wang, inverted wang.

Brain

Back in 1979, while touring with Peaches and Herb, I caught what doctors called "Malaysian Dementia" from a fine little groupie in Patpong. Days after taming that booty, I started experiencing headaches and short blackouts. Two weeks later I awoke in Charles de Gaulle airport wearing a Soviet track and field uniform and carrying several hundred thousand dollars in cash.

Eyes

One evening I approached what I believed to be a common bus station skank, whom I offered the promise of a night on the wang, as they say. Unfortunately, she was both uninterested in my romantic advances and armed with a rather large canister of pepper spray. Eventually I succeeded in

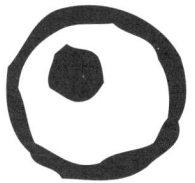
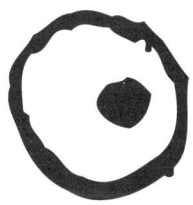

convincing her to allow me to accompany her to the nearest restroom for some smooth sweet action. You can imagine my chagrin when several hours later, my vision cleared enough for me to realize that my companion for the evening was neither a fine lady nor a bus station skank, but a men's room soap dispenser.

Shoulder

While getting to know a young lady's booty in the most biblical of senses, the Ladies Man slipped on the recently disinfected floor of a particular gas station's restroom facilities and knocked my shoulder out of place. While this was exceptionally painful, it did allow me access to a variety of sexual positions heretofore undocumented in the annals of modern "Penthouse" Forums. So this is not really a disease as much as one of the greatest moments of my life.

Knee

During one particular session of lovemaking that could be described as both freaky and deaky, the Ladies Man lost control of his John Deere ride-on lawn tractor and suffered a sprained left knee. Luckily, his lady friend escaped serious injury when her fall was broken by the Mayor McCheese costume she happened to be wearing at the time.

Heart

The Ladies Man will never forget Angela. The one whose eyes sparkled like the moon's reflection on a summer lake. The one whose laughter was sweeter than any songbird's trilling refrain. The one who showed Leon the man he was, and the man he wanted to be. The one who stabbed Leon in the heart with a fork at Shoney's when he forgot his wallet.

Caller #3: Yeah, hi, Ladies Man. Sometimes when I'm in the shower at the gym with a bunch of guys, I get aroused. Is that normal?

Leon Phelps: Yes, basically, that is a normal response. It's natural to have those kind of feelings, but, uh, what I want to know is, uh, how a fine lady like yourself could have such a deep voice?

Caller #3: I'm a man.

Leon Phelps: Well, the first thing I would tell you is to keep that secret to yourself, you know? Um, that is something that you are going to have to live with for the rest of your life, and you can never tell. Thank you, caller. Uh, listen, at this point, I feel that I should say to my viewers that, uh, the Ladies Man does not want any more calls like that. Okay? Because those calls, they disturb the Ladies Man, okay? Thanks very much.

LEON'S NIGHT ON THE TOWN FOR JUST $3.98

By this point, the Ladies Man knows what you're thinking. Leon, you may say, I consider myself an expert wangsman, but I do not possess the extensive fiduciary capabilities of, say, a Bob Lanier or a Rufus Thomas. Fear not, indigent wangateers, Leon Phelps will now show you how to trip the light fantastic on your way to doin' the nasty with the skank of your choice, all for the reasonable sum of $3.98.

Picking Her Up

No matter if I plan to spend under $10 or over $23, the bus station is always the first destination when the Ladies Man seeks the company of the kind of skanks only the most moderately priced

mass transportation can supply. When selecting your escort for the evening, it is imperative to look for the following clues so that you can be sure that the young lady in question is indeed a bus station skank and not a member of law enforcement—or worse, a man. First, make sure that she is not carrying her belongings in anything that is intended for use as luggage. Instead, look for those fine ladies whose personal belongings are contained in garbage bags, empty produce boxes, and handkerchiefs tied to sticks.

Total Cost: $0.00

Wining and Dining

If you're like the Ladies Man, you consider this part of the night most crucial to the achievement of yours, the freakiest of goals. Impress her by taking her to a fancy restaurant, preferably one that does not allow you to pour your own soda. Let her order whatever she wants, and do the same yourself. Now, Ladies Man, you may think, how am I, a modest,

self-employed, adult services entrepreneur, going to afford such a fancy spread? The Ladies Man understands your query and answers it thusly. You are going to want to think ahead and bring a particularly stank piece of refuse and place it delicately into your food shortly before you finish eating. The people who run the fancy restaurant in question will not doubt react poorly to the sight of a Band-Aid or feminine hygienic product in the middle of their prime rib. Kindly accept their offer of a free meal and be on your way.

   Now that you've finished your meal, it's time for a quality apéritif, or as I like to call it, "the booty loosener." Like any good Ladies Man, you should already have at least one bottle of Courvoisier at the ready for yourself. For the fairer sex, who possess a slightly more delicate palate, may I suggest a fine mouthwash such as Scope or Plax to get her in the proper mood for giving it up.

Used Band-Aid: $0.00
Mouthwash: $2.98
Total Cost: $2.98

After-Dinner Entertainment

ow that you have filled yourself with complimentary food and fine intoxicating beverages, it's time to show this skank how a true Ladies Man entertains a lady. I recommend a sojourn to your local cinema, preferably around the back, where they tend not to lock the doors nearest the dumpsters. Once inside, you are free to cuddle closely and, with proper technique, periodically touch her on the boob "by accident"—if you know what I'm saying here, and I think you do. May I suggest a film featuring the curvaceous and voluptuous Ms. Delta Burke to get you in the mood? I think I may.

If, for some strange and inexplicable reason, this does not succeed in getting the two of you in prime humpatory condition, you may need to take evasive action and head directly to your local adult entertainment complex, where slightly racier fare can often be had for the economical price of $0.25. Be warned, a $0.25 film lasts for roughly one minute, so be prepared to have to talk to her for the remaining fifteen/twenty seconds.

Movie: $0.25 × 2
Total Cost: $0.50

Doin' It

I know what you're thinking. Getting your freak on should be the only part of the night that's free, provided you are not accompanied by a professional lady of the night. Remember, aspiring wangist, you are entertaining a fine lady, and you must treat her as such. This means that if the bathroom stall you select is of the pay variety, it is up to you, the gentleman, to pay for it.

Now, some say that variety is the Spice Channel of life and as such may favor more exotic locales for their love-filled grapplings. Now, whereas in the past I have been a proponent of such varied and libidinous localities as tunnel entrances, storm drains, and McDonald's Playland Ball Crawls, I have come to realize that no aphrodisiac known to man has as hornifying an effect on a lady as a Magic Fingers bed. But, Ladies Man, you say, a hotel that features such a device could cost anywhere from $15 to $20. Correct, is my reply. However, your local laundromat features several machines that provide the same bootastical stimulation for a meager $0.25.

And if you are a truly frugal wangulator, may I direct you to the nearest subway exhaust grate, and encourage you to memorize the schedule. Yes, baby, the Earth did just move.

Pay Toilet: $.25
Washing Machine: $.25
Total Cost: $0.50

Getting Rid of Her

No Ladies Man worth his salt will ever allow a lady to return to her home or place of temporary residence without arranging for her transportation. In today's world, it is imperative that you see her all the way home, but more important is that you prevent her from finding out where you live. As such, I suggest convincing her to act really drunk (unless she actually is drunk, in which case, kudos to you, my good man) and arrange for a Sober Cab. This service is provided free to intoxicated drivers in most cities, and, in addition to taking your lady home for the evening, can save you subway fare on your trip back to the bus station.

Total Cost: $0.00

FORMS OF CONTRACEPTION

As a Ladies Man, I am frequently asked about the subject of contraception. Now while I am not exactly sure what that is, I am an expert on both love makin' and baby prevention, so here goes. These are just a few of the questions that I am frequently asked.

1. CONDOMS

When my girlfriend and I have sex, we always use condoms. That's a pretty good form of contraception, right?

Yes, indeed it is, despite the nay-sayers who claim that wearing such prophylactic devices is not dissimilar from wearing a raincoat in the shower. Now, I have paid various professional skanks upwards of $20 to wear not only raincoats in the shower, but also chaps, a navy admiral's uniform, and catcher's gear, all of which I found to be very sexy, so I am not quite sure what this expression means.

I've heard that condoms can break. Should I be concerned about that?

No, not at all. In my experience, all condoms are designed to break or tear away as they are insufficient for accommodating any healthy, normally-sized wang. So keep on doing whatever it is that you're doing.

What's more effective—sheepskin or latex?

Yeah, well, while this is not my area of expertise, I will not criticize you for experimentation — I myself have been drunk too. As for latex, I think that is an explosive.

2. THE PILL

Ladies Man, can you still get pregnant when you're taking the Pill?

Well, you need to be more specific about "the Pill." I absolutely do not recommend having sex with a skank on 'ludes if that is what you mean. Rest assured, though, it can be done. If by "pill" you mean aspirin or cold medication, then, unfortunately,  there is no scientific evidence to prove that these common pharmaceutical products will prevent your sperms from waking up the tiny babies that live in women's stomachs.

3. The Rhythm Method

My girlfriend and I have been using the rhythm method. Is that an effective form of contraception?

Most certainly. I have found that playing particular rhythmic tracks by artists such as Chico DeBarge or, in certain cases, Guy, can greatly enhance the entire love makin' experience.

My girlfriend says that she can figure out when she's ovulating by taking her temperature and writing it down on a calendar.

Yeah, well to the best of my knowledge, "ovulating" is one of the phaser settings on the fine science-fiction program "Star Trek" and as such has little or no bearing on the woman's body. In short, I am certain that your "girlfriend" is lying to you and is probably a man.

4. Showering

Ladies Man, my girlfriend says that showering during or immediately after sex can stop you from having a baby. Is that true?

I would say "yes" as it is very sexy. Regardless of what it does, I would encourage your girlfriend to do it as often as possible, and it would not hurt if she were to don a particularly sexy outfit (see question №1). I would also take photographs.

5. The Infallible Method

Ladies Man, are there any 100 percent effective means of contraception?

Most certainly. The one that I typically employ is scientifically known as the "Uh, yeah, that ain't mine" method. I would like to illustrate this method with this short vignette that I have prepared:

Skank: [She is carrying a baby] Leon, this is your son, Nextelle.

Leon Phelps: Uh, yeah, that ain't mine.

This method has never failed me, Leon Phelps, the Ladies Man.

SELECTED EXCERPTS FROM LEON'S LITTLE BLACK BOOK

ike any self-respecting gentleman of the world, the Ladies Man maintains a comprehensive skankatological catalog of the various ladies that he has had the pleasure of encountering on his journeys of the wang. While some may refer to this document as a "Little Black Book," the Ladies Man's is neither little nor black. Nor is it a book, having long since been catalogued and stored in the Leon Phelps Microfilm Wing of Harvard University's Widener Library.

Stephanie Miller (LC72-83804)[1]
BS[2] 7/16/84,[3] Gem.[4] ☹,[5]
374,[6] PBT/B,[7] .4,[8] 42,[9]
★★★[10]

Alison Hunter (PS3566.Y55C79)GS,[11]
4/10/98,[12] Can.,[13] ☺,[14] D,[15]
PO,[16] F,[17]
16,[18]★★★[19]

??????[20] (PS3566.Y55S5)
??, ??/??/92 (?), ?,
?AL,[21] ??, ??,
????????

Sofonda Coxx (PS3566.Y55V56)
M.[22]

1. In order to deal with the sheer volume of entries, I have adopted the same cataloguing system used by the Library of Congress. To help you understand the magnitude of my archive, the number of ladies who have unclosed their wang-ports to the Ladies Man roughly corresponds to the population Wilkes-Barre, Pennsylvania.

2. This notation refers to the location of our rendezvous, in this case, the bus station. Ladies Man Fun Fact: The Ladies Man meets 75.4 percent of all his ladies at the bus station. That's a lot of ladies!

3. I remember July 16, 1984, as if it were yesterday. I wasn't expecting to fall in love that day, not until this fair princess crossed my path. We did it in the bathroom of the Blimpies outside the Lincoln Tunnel.

4. The Ladies Man is a firm believer in astrology vis a vis the getting of one's freak on. This fine young skank happened to be starolitically governed by the Gemini which, as you know, is the sign of the two gay men. The Ladies Man recommends that you stay away from all Geminis, just in case.

5. As this symbol indicates, this particular lady provided the Ladies Man with a rather delicate venereal inflammation. As an aside, this was the Ladies Man's 100th discrete incidence of herpes and that does represent a personal milestone no matter how you cut it.

6. Our love-making session clocked in at approximately 374 minutes. This tender interlude was cut short only when the night manager informed us that Blimpies was indeed closing.

7. This bit of code refers to distinguishing characteristics, in this case, a Playboy Bunny Tattoo located on the butt. The seasoned wangster can easily identify the various varieties of skank by their

markings. For instance, the bus station species invariably bears the tell-tale Playboy Bunny, typically on the butt, whereas the gas station skank frequently bears the Dixie Stars and Bars also, typically, on the butt.

8. On a scale from 0 to 1, this particular skank rated a ".4" (or, "Kinda Stanky") in the stankiness department. All in all, a thoroughly respectable showing.

9. In order to secure the affections of certain ladies, sometimes the Ladies Man is forced to take on an assumed identity. In this case, I used my forty-second alias, that being the estimable Marlon Jackson of the Jackson 5. Needless to say, they were still hot from the "Victory" tour at the time.

10. Three kids.

11. Gas Station. Ladies Man Fun Fact: The Ladies Man meets 23.9 percent of all his ladies at the gas station. That's some ladies! (What happened to the other .7 percent, you ask? Please kindly consider bail bondsman's offices, check cashiers, and maternity wards.)

12. I remember April 10, 1998, as if it were yesterday. I wasn't expecting to fall in love that day, not until this fair princess crossed my path. We did it in the bathroom of the Popeyes outside of Comiskey Park.

13. Although the Zodiacal sign for Cancer is the crab, the Ladies Man did not contract crabs from this particular lady.

14. This symbol is reserved for ladies who do not successfully transmit a venereal disease to the Ladies Man. It does not appear as frequently as you might think.

15. Drunk.

16. Passed out. Midway through our amative pork session, both of us awakened to realize that we had been passed out for upwards of three hours. Allow me to assuage your fears, dear reader, it's going to take more than a lack of consciousness to de-tumesceticate this wang.

17. Fat.

18. Here the Ladies Man used alias number 16, a personal favorite—Ted Lange also known as Isaac from T.V.'s "Loveboat." Mr. Lange is a sure-fire winner when dealing with ladies cut from a slightly more sophisticated cloth. Suffice it to say this Princess' cruise was "outtasight."

19. Three fingers on right hand.

20. On the evening when I encountered this highly humpable skank, I had perhaps unwisely consumed a cocktail of my own devising which consisted of one part bottle of Courvoisier and one part bottle of cold medication. Suffice it to say, my memories of the night are limited and hazy at best.

21. Artificial leg.

22. This beautiful, statuesque young lady had initially won both the Ladies Man's heart and wang with her buxom figure and colorful pun name. Sadly, she was not a woman at all, but a man wearing a dress.

Charlene: You said you were going to take me to dinner and a movie tonight, Leon.

Leon: Oh yeah... well, um... when I said "dinner," what I meant was, uh, we'd be having sex. And, uh, when I said "movie," I meant we'd be videotaping it.

Killin' Time

LEON'S BERLITZ GUIDE TO WORLD-WIDE CONQUEST

Leon Phelps, the Ladies Man, am what you would call a well-seasoned traveler, being an expert in all things French—including, but not limited to Kissing and Ticklers. I have also heard of Portugal, although I do not swing that way if you know what I mean. While sweet love makin' may be the universal language, it is often difficult to verbally explain one's possession of a superior wang. So here, fellow traveler, is a full list of all you need to know for hours of satisfying international skank humping.

WANG:

French: Le Wang

Italian: Il Wangino

German: Der Wäng (or for you less fortunate types: Das Wängchen)

Spanish: El Wango

Mexican: I've got four dollars.

American Sign Language: WANG!!

Chinese: Wang-Chung

Japanese: Smith

Canadian: Wang, eh

Russian: Wangski

Eskimo: Snow

Ojibwa: Dancing, One-Eyed Trouser Wang

Scottish: McWang

Irish: O'Wang

Arizona: Flagstaff

English: Wang

Dutch: I've got twenty dollars.

LEON'S FIVE SEXIEST NOVELS

1. **LADY CHATTERLEY'S LOVER**
   Now this is an old-timey novel-type book that I have not actually ever read or seen on Cinemax, but every time I hear those three sexy words "Lady," and "Chatterley," and "Lover," I am deeply effected in my wangal region. Next time you are on a bus or in an elevator and you are in search of that first line, lean over and softly say, "Chatterley." You'll see that she will melt at the mere oration of its oratorical bark.

2. **TALE OF TWO CITIES BY READER'S DIGEST**
   The Ladies Man had quite a bit of time to read between the months of April and November 1983 as I was being quarantined under the Federal Emergency Management Act. It seems that certain government agencies that shall remain nameless considered me a Class Four Threat to the state of the national health due to my multitudinous and proliferacious social infirmities. But I digress. This sweeping Victorian epic bridges the two worlds of Jacobean-era Paris and London. I did not find this

to be at all sexy. But then I started imagining the two cities—that is, Paris and London—as two nasty and dirty skanks who were getting their freak on against the backdrop of the tumultuous birthing process of the modern democratic nation state. Outtasight! The book took a strange and decidedly unsexy turn for the worse when it began to tell the story of a white-water rafting trip gone horribly wrong followed by some humorous anecdotes about life in the military.

3. THE BEST OF PENTHOUSE FORUM

This series of thematically linked novellas unquestionably represents the apex of contemporary Western prose. Sadly, this fact has gone unremarked upon by the literary community since its annual publication dating to 1974. The anonymous author of this seminal roman à clef is undoubtedly deserving of numerous and palmary accolades. To this end, I have begun a letter-writing campaign to nominate this author for the Nobel Prize for Literature. Unfortunately, my letters to the so-called "book lovers" at Barnes & Noble Booksellers have yet to induce them to award their prize to this unheralded litérateur.

4. THE WORLD BOOK ENCYCLOPEDIA PRESENTS "R"

Pound for pound this may be the single most sexually exhilarative tome that I have ever had the good fortune to chance upon. As you thumb through R, I suggest that you stop your perusal at both "Reubens" and "Rodin"—two stunning, naked beauties, the latter of which I believe is made out of stone. And of course, the coup de grâce here is the extensive centerfold pictorial, "Reproduction." Frankly, the explicitness and hornifying effect of this stunning spread trumps even the very best of Cheri or, I will go so far as to say, "Black Tail."

5. **BAKIN' WITH THE SUGARBAKERS:**
Delta Burke in the Kitchen. This is ostensibly a cookbook containing hundreds of low-fat, easy-to-prepare recipes, but the only dish the Ladies Man has been able to do in between its covers is a little something called Stiffened Wang à la Suzanne Sugarbaker.

ere are a few other books that I have not read per se, but whose titles nonetheless give me a great deal of wangological contentedness:

HARD TIMES
SUPERFUDGE
GO DOWN, MOSES
THE COLLECTED WORKS OF CHARLES DICKENS
LITTLE WOMEN
THE RAG AND BONE SHOP OF THE SOUL
HOWARDS END
THE TAMING OF THE SHREW
V
PORTRAIT OF A LADY
THE TURN OF THE SCREW
THE ICEMAN COMETH
THE COLLECTED WORKS OF HONORÉ DE BALZAC
OLIVER TWIST
LITTLE MEN
THE COLLECTED WORKS OF EZRA POUND
SONS AND LOVERS
WOMEN IN LOVE
THE COLLECTED WORKS OF LONGFELLOW
IVANHOE

THE PICKWICK PAPERS
THE COLLECTED WORKS OF LOVECRAFT
MOBY DICK
BAG OF BONES
THE WANGTASTIC ADVENTURES OF PROFESSOR WANGDOODLE AND HIS WANGARIFIC WANGAMABOB (BY LEON PHELPS, WORK IN PROGRESS, CURRENTLY UNPUBLISHED)

Leon Phelps: Yeah, yeah, well, The Ladies Man is here to help you. Um... so tell me, uh, how fat are you?

Caller #4: I'm like, 210.

Leon Phelps: Now, that is big. Um, I was not expecting you to say anything over 200 pounds. Uh, I was basically expecting, like, 130, 135... yeah, you are a big woman. Um, my advice to you is to, uh, avoid any type of food product that your neighborhood supermarket might try to sell you. But here's to you, Fat Lady. The Ladies Man loves you, but not in any type of sexual or love-type way.

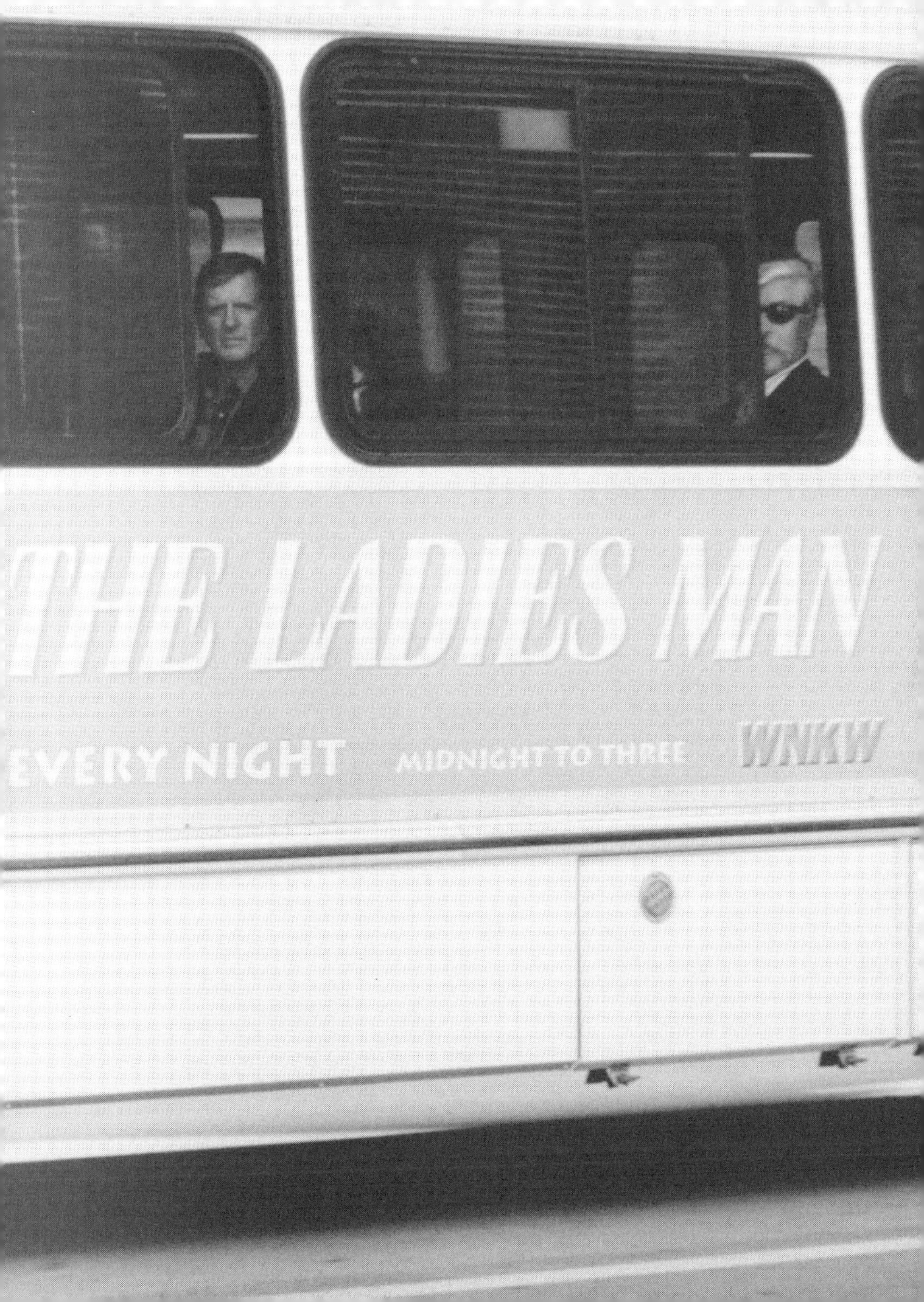
THE LADIES MAN
EVERY NIGHT
MIDNIGHT TO THREE
WNKW

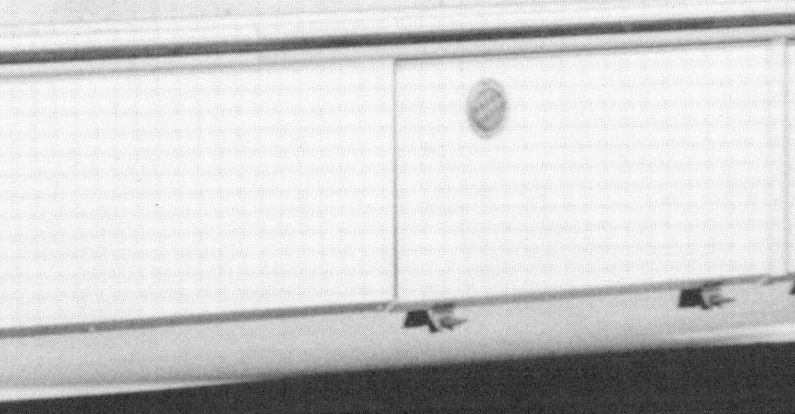

Acknowledgments

To Michelle, Kiki, Alana, Emma, Elizabeth, Gracie, Erik Kenward, Matt Murray, and to Lorne: thanks from Tim, Andrew, and Dennis.